H·E·B read 3

GROW YOUNG MINDS, READ 3 TIMES A WEEK

H-E-B is strongly committed to improving education in Texas and has supported Texas schools through the Excellence in Education Awards program for more than 10 years. In 2011, when H-E-B learned that Texas was facing a major challenge regarding early childhood education and kindergarten readiness, H-E-B started the Read 3 Early Childhood Literacy Campaign.

Read 3's goals are to provide easy and affordable access to books for Texas families and encourage families to read to their early learners at least three times every week. Reading to a child improves his literacy, and when a child's literacy improves, she is more likely to succeed in school, less likely to drop out, and more likely to finish college. That's a brighter future for the child, the family, and for Texas.

Commit to reading at least three times a week to your early learner. Take the Read 3 Pledge!

"A, B, C and 1, 2, 3 – Reading is fun for me.
It helps me grow my young mind.
This week I pledge to read 3 times!"

THIS BOOK BELONGS TO

_____

HI!
I'M BLAZE

One day, Blaze and his driver AJ were at Axle City Garage. Their friend Gabby, the Monster Machine mechanic, was showing them her new delivery: four sets of . . .

"Silly tires!" Gabby proclaimed.

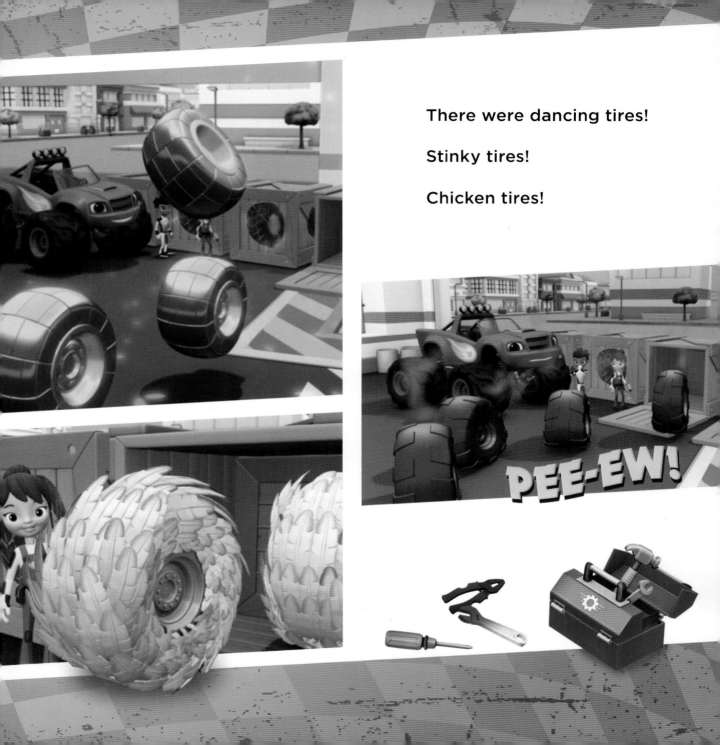

There were dancing tires!

Stinky tires!

Chicken tires!

PEE-EW!

Before Gabby could open the fourth crate, Zeg the dinosaur truck slowly pulled up. Zeg was having trouble driving. He had four flat tires full of holes and rips!

"I've got some tires for you," said Gabby.

"We'll be right back!" said Blaze as he, Gabby, and AJ went to find the perfect tires for Zeg.

Suddenly, the fourth crate popped open—and out bounced four green tires!

"Funny tires go up and down!" said Zeg. "Zeg like! Zeg want those tires."

Zeg tried on the new tires. Wow!

"Zeg bouncing!" he called. "Waa-ha!"

Gabby looked worried. "Blaze, AJ," she said, "we have a problem. Those tires are the silliest tires of them all. They're Super Bouncy Tires. Once those Super Bouncy Tires start bouncing, they don't stop!"

"Whoa-oa!" cried Zeg. "Tires not stopping! Zeg still bouncing! Whoa!!!"

Zeg bounced and flipped and bounced—right out of the garage and down the street!

"AJ and I will find a way to stop those bouncy tires," declared Blaze.

"To catch Zeg, we've got to use some BLAZING speed!" added AJ.

"Look! There he is!"
cried Blaze.

Boing Boing! Zeg just kept bouncing through the town, right into a fountain and a clothesline!

WHOOPSIE! ZEG GOT PANTS ON FACE!

"Poor Zeg!" said Blaze.

"This is a big problem," said AJ. "And to help our friend, we've got to find a solution."

"I know how we can save Zeg," offered Blaze. "Let's make those bouncy tires stick to the road. We'll use adhesion. Adhesion is when two different things stick together."

"Oh, yeah!" said AJ. "We can use something sticky like . . .

. . .tape! Darington! He has tape! Hey, Darington. Can we use your tape?"

"Sure! Anything for you, Blaze!"

"Thanks, Darington!"

They rolled out the sticky tape. Things stick to tape, and when two things stick together, that's adhesion!

"Quick! Here he comes!" called AJ.

But would the tape make those bouncy tires stick?

Boing! Boing! Plop! S-t-r-e-t-c-h . . .

WHOA!

—*SNAP!*

The tape was not sticky enough.

"Next time we try adhesion, we have to use something even stickier," said AJ.

Blaze and AJ zoomed after Zeg

Zeg boinged and bounced away. He bounced right through an egg warehouse—without breaking an egg! Then he crashed into a shoe stand!

ZEG HAVE SHOE ON NOSE

"We need something *really* sticky to make those tires stick to the road," said AJ. "Like glue!"

AJ squirted a big puddle of glue on the road—and here came Zeg! Would the glue make those bouncy tires stick?

Boing! Boing! Boing!—

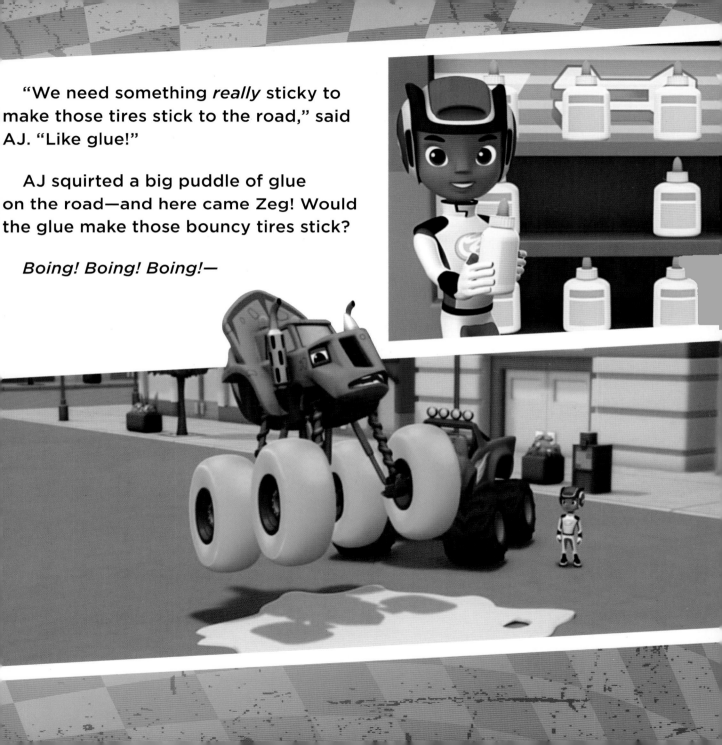

—*Plop! S-t-r-e-t-c-h . . . SNAP!*

The glue was not sticky enough.

"To stop those tires, we're going to need something even *stickier*!" said AJ.

Blaze and AJ raced after the bouncing Monster Machine. They see construction workers using cement as adhesion.

Down the street, Crusher and Pickle were bored sitting in traffic. Zeg bounced into the air and over the traffic!

"Aw, how come *he* gets to have Super Bouncy Tires?" whined Crusher. "Come on, Pickle. I'm gonna get those tires!"

Crusher shot out a towline and latched onto Zeg—sending Crusher bouncing out of control!

"Don't worry, Crusher. I'll save you!" Pickle said as he latched on, too.

The three Monster Machines bounced and screamed down the road, until—*SPLAT!*—Crusher and Pickle crashed into some paint cans.

Zeg missed the paint cans and kept bouncing down the street toward the bakery. Oh, no! He was headed straight for a great big cake!

"Somebody stop him!" cried the baker!

"Gaskets!" exclaimed Blaze. "We need to stop those bouncy tires—and fast!"

"This is our last chance to use adhesion!" said AJ.

"I've got an idea," said Blaze. "What if we use quick-dry cement?"

"Cement is really great for adhesion," agreed AJ, "because when it dries, it gets really hard. But to make cement, we're gonna need . . . a cement mixer!"

"Come on!" cheered Blaze. "We can turn me into a cement mixer! We need a SPIRAL MIXING BLADE to stir the ingredients! A ROTATING DRUM to mix the cement! Last we need a DISCHARGE CHUTE to pour out the cement!"

I'M A CEMENT-MIXING MMMONSTER MACHINE!

Blaze raced past Zeg! The cement was ready! This was their last chance to stop those bouncy tires!

Zeg came bounding down the street. Would the cement make those bouncy tires stick?

Boing! Boing! Boing!—

SPLAT! Yes! "No more boingy bouncing!" said Zeg with relief.

"Woo-hoo!" cheered Blaze. "We found the solution to our problem just in time."

"Quick-dry cement is adhesive enough to stop bouncy tires," added AJ.

"Zeg thank Blaze and AJ," said Zeg. "You save Zeg!"

"You're welcome, big fella. Now, let's go get you a different set of tires."

"There ya go, Zeg," said Gabby after tightening the last lug nut.

"New tires good!" said Zeg. "Look. No bouncing!"

And where did those Super Bouncy Tires go? Reese hauled them off to the recycling plant.

SO LONG, BOUNCY TIRES!